For Suzy – P. C.

To my Babcia, Elizabeth Sadowska, 28.2.1926 - 27.6.2007 – N. R.

First American Edition 2010
Kane Miller, A Division of EDC Publishing

First published in 2008 by Working Title Press, Australia
Text copyright © Phil Cummings 2008
Illustrations copyright © Nina Rycroft 2008

For information contact:
Kane Miller, A Division of EDC Publishing
P.O. Box 470663
Tulsa, OK 74147-0663
www.kanemiller.com
www.edcpub.com

Library of Congress Control Number: 2009931230

Manufactured by Regent Publishing Services, Hong Kong
Printed September 2010 in ShenZhen, Guangdong, China
1 2 3 4 5 6 7 8 9 10

ISBN: 978-1-935279-22-8

Boom Bah!

Kane Miller
A DIVISION OF EDC PUBLISHING

Ting!

Shhh! Listen!
What's that sound?

Tong!

Shhh! Listen!
Gather round.

A bell, a can,
Some lids, a cup.

Ting! Tong!
Warming up.

A box, a bowl,
A spoon, a stick.

Tap! Tap!
Clickety-click!

Shhh! Listen!
I hear more.

One, two, three, four!

Nod your head.

Tap your toe.

BOOM BAH!

Here we go!

Bing! Bong!
Up and down!

Clickety-click!
Round and round!

Look! There!

Another crowd!

BOOM BAH!

Very loud!

Hey ho! Clap your hands!

Hey ho! Join the band!

Tra-la-la!
Ring! Ring!

Tra-la-la!
Sing! Sing!

All together! One, two, three!

All together ... follow me!

Hey ho! …

Tah-dah!

Ting! Tra-la-la! Sing! Sing! Ring! Ring!

Bong! Bing! Tong! Tra-la-la! Sing! Sing! Bong!

Tong! Tap! Tap!

Ring! Ring! Tra-la-la! Sing! Sing! Clickety-click!

Ting!

Bing! Tap! Tap! Tong! Bong!

Tra-la-la! Sing! Sing! Ring! Ring! Ting!